This igloo book belongs to:

....

igloobooks

Published in 2019
by Igloo Books Ltd
Cottage Farm
Sywell
NN6 0BJ
www.igloobooks.com

GOL002 0319
2 4 6 8 10 9 7 5 3 1
ISBN 978-1-78905-661-7

Written by Sienna Williams
Illustrated by Nicola Anderson

Designed by Matthew Ellero
Edited by Caroline Richards

Printed and manufactured in China

There was a contest in the
jungle and auditions were at 8.
The singers were all rehearsing
and Hilda Hippo couldn't wait.

The host appeared on stage
and the audience began to **cheer.**
"Welcome to Jungle Idol!" he cried.
"The competition starts right here!"

Each act sang for the judges
and they got a yes or no.

The
Bass Bullfrogs
impressed and got through
to the final show.

The **Disco Chimps** amazed.

The **La-La-Lions** sounded sweet.

But the judges said the **Rockin' Crocs** were the ones to beat.

Next Hilda went on stage
to sing her heart out with her song.
The first two lines were **perfect**…
and then it all went wrong.

"I'm sorry," said the head judge,
"you just don't have what it takes.
You've got musical talent,
but you made too many mistakes."

Hilda hung her head and sighed as she **plodded** on her way.

"I'll win that singing contest," she said, "no matter what they say!"

The auditions carried on and Hilda found a place to sing.
She made herself a makeshift stage where no one would hear a thing.

"TRAA-LA-LA!"

she **belted** out, at the top of her lungs.

"YEAH, YEAH, OO-OO-OO!"

It was the **best** she'd ever sung.

Then, down from the trees, flew Parrot, Toucan and Cockatoo. "Wow!" they said together. "We all wish we could sing like you."

"You sing beautifully," said Hilda. She always heard them **squawk** in-tune. But they knew Hilda had something special. She'd be a superstar soon.

"You were probably just nervous," said Toucan, "singing all alone."
"We'll sing backup with you," said Parrot, "so you won't be on your own!"

So Hilda and her friends practised long into the night.

Their notes were all **pitch-perfect**...

... and their harmonies just right.

When the final came,
the contestants all gathered backstage.
They saw Hilda's brand new super-group
and flew into a **rage**.

"You can't be here," they said.
"Last time you messed up every note!
Compete against our groups
and you won't get one single vote."

But Hilda Hippo was greeted warmly, when she got up to perform.
The judges gave her a second chance to take the jungle crowd by storm.

She sang like an angel, with her **squawking** back-up team.
She **strutted** like a diva. It went better than a dream.

When the votes had all been counted, Hilda closed her eyes.
"The winner of Jungle Idol is… Hilda!" said the host, to her surprise.

"I couldn't have done it without my friends," said Hilda, taking a bow.
"You just needed your confidence back," they said. "You're a big star now!"